A Story

Sentences can tell a story.

Read the sentences. Match each sentence to the right picture. Write the number in the box.

Henry Hippo

1. Henry Hippo likes to swim.
   He needs a big lake.

2. Henry jumps into the lake.
   The water splashes everywhere.

3. His friends say good-bye.
   The water is gone.

Draw a Picture

Read the sentences. Draw a picture for each sentence. Look for the words that will help you make the picture.

1. The brown dog sees the red ball.

2. Tom runs to the big green tree.

3. The blue car stops at my house.

Skill: understanding sentences

Which Word Is Right?

Draw a circle around the right word to finish each sentence.

1. The box has a (top tap).	1.
2. Can (us you) see my doll?	2.
3. (Was Saw) the book good?	3.
4. The truck is (from fast).	4.
5. I (can come) run, too.	5.
6. The pig can (dug dig).	6.

Skill: completing sentences using the correct word

3

Which Word Is Right?

Draw a circle around the right word to finish each sentence. Write it on the line.

1. Tom will go _____.
(house home)

2. I am _____ after you.
(runs running)

3. Please come with _____.
(me my)

4. We will _____ cookies.
(make made)

5. _____ book is mine.
(These This)

4

One Word Too Many

Draw a circle around the right word to finish each sentence.

1. Is (my   for) mother here?

2. I (up   can) play with my pet.

3. We (went   saw) to the park.

4. Jan (have   will) go with us.

5. Ben put the car (some   away).

6. The cow (gives   stop) milk.

7. Did you (find   ride) in the wagon?

Make a Poem

You can have fun with words. Read these words that rhyme. Choose some words for your poem. Write them on the lines.

bat	fat	mat	rat	pat
cat	hat	vat	sat	flat

My Poem

_____

There was a big _____

that sat on a _____

and grew very _____.

Draw a picture about your poem.

Spotting Sentences

What is a sentence?
A sentence must make sense. It is a complete thought.
This is not a sentence. <u>the fish</u>
This is a sentence. <u>**The fish can swim.**</u>

◀ Put an <u>X</u> on the line if the words make a sentence.

_____ up the hill

_____ The dog ran up the hill.

_____ I made a game.

_____ made a game

_____ the girl

_____ The girl saw a bird.

_____ My house is blue.

_____ my blue house

_____ Jim plays ball.

_____ my brother Jim

Bright Ideas

What do you notice about these sentences?

Using Capital Letters

All sentences must start with a capital letter.

Draw a circle around the right word to finish each sentence. Write it on the line.

1.	______ I go?	May may
2.	______ big tree is green.	the The
3.	______ can swim fast.	Fish fish
4.	______ bird will sing.	A a
5.	______ can run and jump.	Dogs dogs
6.	______ are very slow.	Turtles turtles
7.	______ house is white.	my My

Runaway Capitals

Sentences and names begin with <u>capital letters</u>.

 These sentences have mistakes. Write the sentences on the lines. Put in the capital letters.

1. is tom running fast?

Is Tom running fast?

2. i play with sue.

3. my name is josh.

4. did sarah read?

5. you get a sticker!

Put a sticker here.

Stop Signals

These are stop signals for sentences. ! ? .

Sentences need a way to stop. A <u>statement</u> is one kind of sentence. It **tells** us something. A statement ends with a <u>period</u> (.).

Draw a line from each picture to a word. Write the word on the line. Put a period (.) at the end of each sentence.

runs

eats

barks

The dog eats.

laughs

sings

jumps

The clown

hides

sleeps

plays

The dragon

hops

eats

is green

The monster

<u>Skill:</u> using periods to end sentences

Stop Signals

These are stop signals for sentences. ! ? .

Sentences need a way to stop. A <u>question</u> is a sentence that **asks** something. A <u>question</u> ends with a <u>question mark</u> (?).

Read the sentences. Put a question mark (?) at the end of each sentence.

May I ride with you _____
Will the cat run away _____
What are you doing _____
When will you call me _____

Draw a line to make a question.

1. Did you	your name?
2. Where is my	see the elephant?
3. What is	the party start?
4. When will	new bike?

I Can Do It!

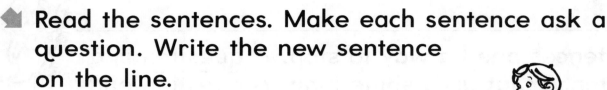 Read the sentences. Make each sentence ask a
question. Write the new sentence
on the line.

1. John can run.

Can John run?

2. Tom will jump.

_____

3. Jill can read.

_____

4. Dan is swinging.

_____

5. Ann will help her mother.

_____

Skill: writing questions

I Can Do It!

Read the sentences. Change each question to a sentence that is a statement.

1. Will Roger sing?

Roger will sing.

2. Can Bill play?

- - - - - - - - - - -

3. Is the food hot?

- - - - - - - - - - -

4. Is Lee running?

- - - - - - - - - - -

5. Will my father work?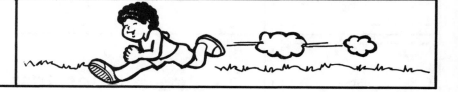

- - - - - - - - - - -

Nouns

A <u>noun</u> is a word that names a person, animal, place or thing.

Find a noun to finish each sentence. Write the letter on the line. Find the matching stickers.

sticker	1. The _____ is hot.	A. Bill
sticker	2. _____ reads a book.	B. bus
sticker	3. The _____ is loud.	C. sun

sticker	4. A _____ can fly.	D. bike
sticker	5. _____ runs fast.	E. bird
sticker	6. The _____ can roll.	F. Ann
sticker	7. The _____ is new.	G. ball

Finding Nouns

 Look at each picture. Draw a circle around the right noun to finish each sentence.

A. The_____ is playing.

1. boat　　2. cat　　3. ball

B. The_____ are fun.

1. toys　　2. car　　3. cow

C. The_____ is little.

1. fish　　2. bird　　3. dog

D. The_____ is swimming.

1. sun　　2. fish　　3. fan

Skill: using picture clues to select nouns

Special Nouns

Names are special nouns. All names must start with a capital letter.

◀ Read the sentences. Write the name on the line.

_____

My name is _____•

My friend's name is _____•

The name of my city is _____•

◀ Think of a name for each pet. Write it on the line.

cat _____

dog _____

<u>Skill:</u> understanding proper nouns

Press out stickers, moisten, and place them on the pages where they belong.

page 14

pages 28 and 29

Use these stickers as rewards on any page.

super neat

Rewards!

WAY TO GO!

GR·R·REAT

GOOD WORK!!

Alright

More Rewards!

Pronouns in Sentences

Pronouns are words used in place of nouns.

Here are some pronouns.

I   he   she   it   you   we   they

Read the first sentence. The noun has a line under it. Read the next sentence. Draw a circle around the pronoun that is used in place of the noun.

Bill wants a boat.
1. (He) sees a sailboat.

1.   sticker

See Pam playing.
2. Can she jump rope?

2.   sticker

Lee will come home.
3. He will take the train.

3.   sticker

Tim and Dan have fun.
4. They play ball.

4.   sticker

Kim and I can run fast.
5. Can we win the race?

5.   sticker

Can you think of a sentence with a pronoun?

Skill: understanding pronouns

17

Finding Action Verbs

A word that tells an action is a <u>verb.</u> The action verb tells you what is happening.

Write the missing action verb on the line to finish each sentence.

action verbs

jump	playing	looking	called
calling	looks	jumped	plays

_____

1. The cat is _____ with the toy.

2. The dog _____ at the turtle.

3. Mother _____ me in to eat.

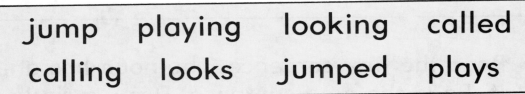
Come and eat!

4. The frog will _____ from the rock.

<u>Skill:</u> understanding action verbs

Using Action Verbs

Draw a circle around the word that will make the **most** sense in each sentence. Write it on the line.

1. The frog is _____.

   (cooking   hopping)

2. My dog is _____.

   (petting   digging)

3. This baby is _____.

   (crying   barking)

4. The jet is _____.

   (singing   flying)

Choose one of the sentences. Draw a picture about the sentence.

Helping Words in Sentences

Write a helping word on the line to finish each sentence.

_____

_____

1. The girls _____ jumping.

_____

2. The girl _____ jumping.

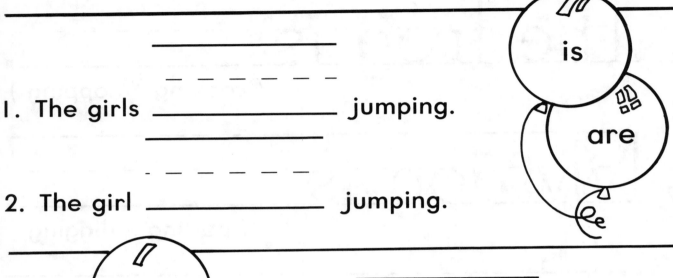

3. He _____ going fast.

4. We _____ going fast.

5. He _____ the dog.

6. I _____ the dog.

7. We have _____ the dog.

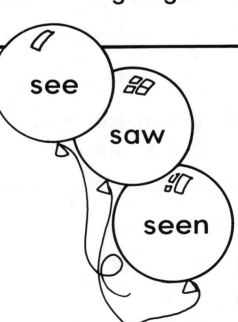

📎 Read the words. Draw a circle around the ones that tell about the picture.

lake	car	store	play
sand	boat	school	sun
city	trees	beach	cat
picnic	dog	read	swim

📎 Write a sentence about the picture. Use some of the words you circled.

_____

_ _

_____

_ _

_____

Did your sentence start with a capital letter?

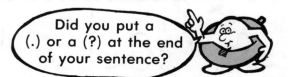

Did you put a (.) or a (?) at the end of your sentence?

Skill: reviewing sentence writing skills

Short Sentences

Look at the pictures. Read the words. Draw a line from each noun to a verb to make a short sentence.

	nouns	verbs
	Fish	trot.
	Girls	swim.
	Horses	bark.
	Dogs	laugh.

	nouns	verbs
	Snakes	grow.
	Flowers	cry.
	Frogs	wiggle.
	Babies	hop.

Skill: combining nouns and verbs to form simple sentences

Making Sentences

A sentence must make sense.

 Draw a line to the best ending.

1. The duck   went up in the air.

2. My puppy   is quacking at me.

3. The balloon   will bark.

4. The bees   will read the book.

5. Ann and Mike   is in the garden.

6. The rabbit   are buzzing.

Find a sentence you like. Write it on the lines.

_____

_ _ _ _ _ _ _ _ _ _ _ _ _ _ _ _ _

_____

Skill: matching subjects and predicates of sentences

23

Growing Sentences

Read the sentences. Choose words from the word bank to make each sentence grow. Write them on the lines.

1. The fish can swim.

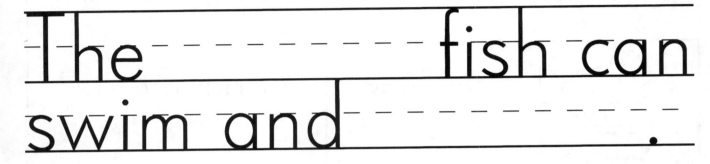

The _____ fish can swim and _____ .

2. I see a tree.

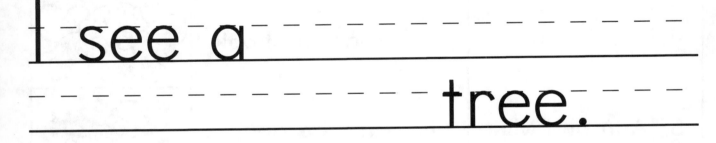

I see a _____ tree.

3. My elephant is fat.

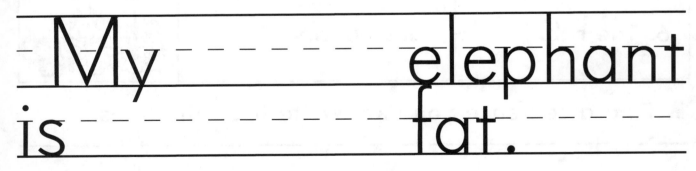

My _____ elephant is fat.

word bank

small   big   eat   very
orange   jump   brown   green

24

Mystery Sentence

Draw a circle around the right word to finish each sentence.

1. Let (I   Tom) have the ball.

2. She saw a (red   will) book.

3. I see the dog (swim   run) up up the hill.

4. Will (the   with) girl come too?

5. The (cat   you) jumps high.

Make a mystery sentence. Write the five words you <u>did not</u> circle on the lines.

_____   _____   _____

1.   2.   3.

_____   _____•

4.   5.

Picture This!

Sentences can tell us to do something.

◀ Read the sentences. Follow the directions.

1. Draw three circles for a snowman.

2. Put a hat on it.

3. Give it eyes and a nose.

4. Make three buttons.

5. Draw a scarf.

6. Give it a smile!

1. Draw an animal you like.

2. Make a home for it.

3. Put a sun in the sky.

4. Draw yourself in the picture.

5. Give yourself a sticker!

26

<u>Skill:</u> following directions

Scrambled Sentences

Read the words. Write the words in a sentence that makes sense.

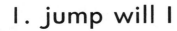 can run I fast
I can run fast.

1. jump will I

_____

_____•

2. sees the dog He

_____

_____•

3. castle a Jane made

_____

_____•

4. are We fast going

_____

_____•

Riddles for You

▸ Read the riddles. Use the word bank on the next page to help you finish each riddle. Write the words on the lines.

▸ Find the sticker that shows what the sentence tells about.

1. It has fur like a cat.

   It does not smell good.

   We <u>smell</u> it with our

   _____

   _____.   It is a ☞

   Put a sticker here.

2. It is fun to make.

   It is sweet to taste.

   We <u>taste</u> it in our

   _____

   _____.   It is a ☞

   Put a sticker here.

3. It has feathers.

   We hear it sing.

   We <u>hear</u> it with our

   _____

   _____.   It is a ☞

   Put a sticker here.

28

More Riddles

Read the riddles. Use the word bank to help you finish each riddle. Write the words on the lines.

Find the sticker that shows what the sentence tells about.

4. The sun helps it grow.

   It has pretty colors.

   We <u>see</u> it with our

   _____

   _ _ _ _ _ _ _ _ _

   _____ .   It is a ☞

   > Put a sticker here.

5. It is wet to touch.

   It can swim.

   We <u>touch</u> it with our

   _____

   _ _ _ _ _ _ _ _ _

   _____ .   It is a ☞

   > Put a sticker here.

word bank

eyes   hands

noses   ears

mouths

<u>Skill:</u> using sentence clues to complete riddles   29

Sentence Sequence

Sentences can tell a story.

◀ Read the sentences. They are not in the right order. Write the sentences so the story makes sense.

Chris ate two cookies.
Mom baked cookies.
Chris put the rest away.

_____

_____

_____

◀ Put the pictures in order. Write the number in the box.

Skill: sequencing sentences

Make Your Own Sentences

Use one word from each colored box. Write the word in the matching ⬚------⬚. Make as many sentences as you can.

noun	helping word	verb
Sue	does	play
Dan	can	jump
Mom	will	color
She	can not	read
He	will not	run

1. _____ _____ _____

2. _____ _____ _____

3. _____ _____ _____

4. _____ _____ _____

5. _____ _____ _____

6. _____ _____ _____

Bright Ideas
Use another sheet of paper to write more sentences.

ANSWERS

Page 1

1	
3	2

Page 3
1. top
2. you
3. Was
4. fast
5. can
6. dig

Page 4
1. home
2. running
3. me
4. make
5. This

Page 5
1. my
2. can
3. went
4. will
5. away
6. gives
7. ride

Page 6
Answers will vary.

Page 7
The dog ran up the hill.
I made a game.
The girl saw a bird.
My house is blue.
Jim plays ball.

⭐ The sentences begin with a capital letter and end with a period.

Page 8
1. May
2. The
3. Fish
4. A
5. Dogs
6. Turtles
7. My

Page 9
2. I play with Sue.
3. My name is Josh.
4. Did Sarah read?
5. You get a sticker!

Page 10
The clown sings.
The dragon sleeps.
The monster eats.

Page 11
1. Did you see the elephant?
2. Where is my new bike?
3. What is your name?
4. When will the party start?

Page 12
2. Will Tom jump?
3. Can Jill read?
4. Is Dan swinging?
5. Will Ann help her mother?

Page 13
2. Bill can play.
3. The food is hot.
4. Lee is running.
5. My father will work.

Page 14
1. C 5. F
2. A 6. G
3. B 7. D
4. E

Page 15
A. 2
B. 1
C. 3
D. 2

Page 16
Answers will vary.

Page 17
2. she
3. He
4. They
5. we

Page 18
1. playing
2. looks
3. called
4. jump

Page 19
1. The frog is hopping.
2. My dog is digging.
3. This baby is crying.
4. The jet is flying.

Page 20
1. are
2. is
3. was
4. were
5. saw
6. see
7. seen

Page 21
lake   dog
sand   beach
picnic   play
boat   sun
trees   swim

Bottom: Answers will vary.

Page 22
Fish swim.
Girls laugh.
Horses trot.
Dogs bark.
Snakes wiggle.
Flowers grow.
Frogs hop.
Babies cry.

Page 23
1. The duck is quacking at me.
2. My puppy will bark.
3. The balloon went up in the air.
4. The bees are buzzing.
5. Ann and Mike will read the book.
6. The rabbit is in the garden.

Page 24
Answers will vary.

Page 25
1. Tom
2. red
3. run
4. the
5. cat

I will swim with you.
1. 2. 3. 4. 5.

Page 27
1. I will jump.
2. He sees the dog.
3. Jane made a castle.
4. We are going fast.

Pages 28 and 29

word	sticker
1. noses	skunk
2. mouths	cupcake
3. ears	bird
4. eyes	flower
5. hands	fish

Page 30
Mom baked cookies.
Chris ate two cookies.
Chris put the rest away.

Bottom:

2	1	3

Page 31
Answers will vary.